## Diggin' Fo' Square Roots

**The Complete Pogo Comics**
**Volume 3: Diggin' Fo' Square Roots**
Eclipse Books, P.O. Box 1099, Forestville, California 95436
First Edition
Clothbound Limited Edition: ISBN 1-56060-037-3
Trade Paperback: ISBN 1-56060-038-1


Dean Mullaney
Publisher

Catherine Yronwode
Editor-in-Chief

Mark Burstein
Editor

Greg Theakston and Miyako Graham
Art Restoration

Visual Strategies, San Francisco
Cover Design

Steve Vance
Logo Design

Jamison Color Prepress
Colour Separations

Jan Mullaney
Chairman

Bruce Palley
Vice-President

Sean Deming
Circulation

Beau Smith
Sales Manager

SPECIAL THANKS TO

Steve Thompson
for advice and the loan of materials used
in the preparation of this volume,

and

Stan Woch
for dextrous use of white paint and brush
in the service of history

# TABLE OF CONTENTS

# Swamp Gas

BY MARK BURSTEIN, SERIES EDITOR

In this, the third volume of *The Complete Pogo Comics,* we are delighted to have such a personal and personable introduction by Malcolm Whyte. He is the founder and director of San Francisco's Cartoon Art Museum, a nonprofit organization dedicated to the collection, preservation and exhibition of original cartoon art in all forms*.

Speaking of prefaces, since our list of introducers came out in Volume II, we have added Kelly's assistant George Ward, author/humorist Cyra McFadden (*The Serial*), and two of Walt's relatives—his widow and executrix, Selby, and his eldest son, Peter.

Eclipse Books is also happy to announce the reprinting of my *Much Ado* (The Pogofenokee Trivia Book) in a revised and expanded edition. A profound bargain at $4.95, it is available directly from Eclipse, or better comic stores everywhere.

Herein, much is developing. The characters are still speaking with a deep South patois (and abominable grammar, even by Okefenokee standards). These stories feature a growing cast of characters, some of who never appear again—Cousin Down-wind (a skunk), Citronella Jones, Aig Haid Noonan—and others who are later transformed into familiar players—Legerdemain Z. Presto (Seminole Sam), the mailman duck (Choo Choo Curtis), Haoun' Dawg (Beauregard Bugleboy), and a large bear (Barnstable). Porkypine makes a brief appearance, and Churchy and Howland have acquired names and distinctive hats.

We are again printing Kelly's charming covers for these *Animal Comics,* which portray Uncle Wiggly as well as the Pogo gang. The last page of this volume reproduces the unusual back cover of *Animal Comics* #20, which portrays a fierce Albert looking like one of the dancing alligators in *Fantasia* (which Kelly helped to animate), and Uncle Wiggly looking like the Bre'r Rabbit Molasses bunny.

'Til next issue...Pozza Mozza Wobble Dee Day!

* For visiting, publication, and membership information write to the Cartoon Art Museum, 665 Third Street, San Francisco, California 94107

# The Cartoon Art of Walt Kelly
## or, Pogo: Why I Love 'im

BY MALCOLM WHYTE

Little did I know as a kid in the 1940s, reading almost every comic book that came off the press, that one day I'd be writing about one of my favorite cartoon artists, Walt Kelly. Nor did I realize then, enjoying *Animal Comics, Fairy Tale Parade*, and *Our Gang*, that it was in fact Walt Kelly's (unsigned) art that drew me to them. But I loved 'em.

I was always fascinated with cartoons and cartooning. I liked to draw a lot. In the sixth grade I crayoned six issues of my creation, Super Bunny, a parody of "Hoppy the Marvel Bunny," which was itself Fawcett Publishing's in-house parody of their own Captain Marvel. By junior high I had lost interest in comic books, except for some of the gorier ECs, but in college two great things happened. I began drawing cartoons for the *Cornell Widow*, the campus humor magazine, and I got thoroughly engrossed in *Pogo*, which was being published in the school's newspaper *The Cornell Daily Sun* (or *The Cornell Deadly Sin*, as we at the *Widow* called it).

Campus life and *Pogo*'s sophisticated humor were perfectly matched during those years. Everyone read the strip. "I Go Pogo" buttons proliferated. Walt Kelly even made a guest appearance in the November 1953 issue of the *Widow*. Amid the godawful jokes ("'I've just lost my best pupil,' quipped the professor as his eyeball rolled down the sink.") were a large, bold drawing of Pogo on the cover and a double page drama inside featuring Kelly in dialogue with his characters. I had a small drawing on page 11.

Imagine Walt Kelly and me in the same magazine! This event focused my attention on his art even more, and, so to speak, inked in my sketchy interest in becoming a cartoonist. As it turned out, I never did. Instead, I got married, had three children, founded—and, twenty-five years later, sold—Troubador Press, and then started the Cartoon Art Museum in San Francisco.

As a collector of cartoon art, I knew how exciting it is to see original works. Inspired by Mort Walker's museum in New York, I thought there should be a place on the West Coast where the public could view original cartoon art, and where such art could be preserved. After five years of planning and touring exhibitions, the Cartoon Art Museum opened its permanent gallery in March of 1988. Our first exhibition there was "Drawn to Excellence: Masters of Cartoon Art" which displayed seventy-five of the finest pieces of newspaper strip, comic book, magazine gag, and animation art available. An original Sunday *Pogo* was the big favorite. Visitors seeing the full-size original remarked how thrilled they were, and how much they loved and missed Kelly's work.

As a critic of the art community might say, "Kelly's adroit calligraphic style manifests a poignant satire on the human condition performed by an iconic, if not totemically imbued, cross-cultural *dramatis personae* of anthropomorphic creatures for amused followers of the fourth estate." To which Pogo would no doubt reply "Hol' everthin'. That's ree-dickledockle. Mr. Kelly jes' draws us for fun! Natural he's good at it. Nobody more artistical. But any totem poll will show he sho 'nuff never been cross or cultural a day in his life!"

So what is it that makes his art so special? Why is he so universally recognized as a master of cartoon art? Let's look at the elements of his style—the setting, characters, action, and purpose—to arrive at an answer.

## The Setting

*Pogo* takes place in a peaceful, naturally beautiful section of the Okefenokee Swamp. Solid, graceful trees draped with soft mosses and gently trailing vines border the placid waters. Now and then elegant waterfowl perch nearby or glide smoothly across the background.

Pogo's and Miz Beaver's houses are plainly cozy. Mr. Miggle's store has a woodsy, country charm. In this tranquil setting, mildly malevolent elements like Simple J. Malarkey and Deacon Mushrat seem all the more sinister in contrast.

The cartoon panels are embraced by an almost organic frame, accommodating enough to be broken by arms, legs, speech balloons, and occasional explosions. Everything is rendered in fluid thick-and-thin brush lines stroked with the confidence of an expert draftsman. Kelly sets a wonderfully imaginative, yet completely believable, stage for his playful cast of characters.

## The Characters

Like Shakespeare, Kelly gives every character, even the most minor, a distinct personality. We get to know them very quickly, and understand that they are complex individuals, far more than two-dimensional devices with which to string out gags. Their identities are revealed in their words, actions, and dress, and solidified by Kelly's (pretty much) consistent delineation.

Pogo is the steady, warm, friendly naif. Albert is a volcanic dreamer who throws himself into any big idea that comes along. His long, lanky-legged body, mobile arms, and large, expressive face perfectly suit his histrionics. Miz Mam'zelle's sexy yet practical glamour radiate from a shapely, fluffy, *tres* French skunk. Miz Beaver is a busy, capable, caring mother. Even my favorites, the bat brothers, Bewitched, Bothered, and Bemildred, have different natures, although they themselves can never quite tell which of them is who.

Kelly has fashioned a rich variety of characters, down to the smallest bug or tad, who act and react to each other in hilarious sequences.

### The Action

In *Pogo* an idea is always emerging and we wonder just what these nutty characters are going to do next. Whether they are sitting quietly or running amok, there's a liveliness to the figures seldom seen in other cartoon art.

The quiet activity of resting on a log, fishing from a barge, or ambling about may anticipate developing action or pithy conversation that soon becomes plot. The players' deftly animated bodies lean, slump, or pitch with appropriate balance and weight. Kelly knew exactly how bones and muscles move.

When the action speeds up, the characters almost fly off the page. With a "ploomp", "bang!", or "whoop!!" they burst through the panels in a riotous romp of slapstick born of misunderstanding or high adventure gone awry.

The action is usually motivated by the characters' idiosyncrasies. It's classically funny stuff, brought to life by cartoon art's premier genius.

### The Purpose

Every artist is a communicator and has a point to make. Walt Kelly seeks to move us—primarily to spontaneous laughter, secondarily to thought. In the *Pogo* strips the timing, from first to last panel, is flawless. In the case of the longer comic book stories, although there may be several highlights along the way, we can be sure of a delicious payoff at the punchline.

The points he makes play so well because we recognize that human nature—for better or worse—is behind them all. We have met the Okefenokee gang, and they is us. Upon occasion, when he feels that it is important to unstuff some political or ecclesiastical shirt, Kelly turns his wit from exposing human folly in general to satirizing specific individuals. And sometimes he even tweaks himself, as in an early strip where Porkypine shuffles off the last panel mumbling, "sometimes the humor of this strip eludes me."

Of course, the humor of *Pogo* never escapes us. Nor does the buoyancy of its characters, the color, the strength, and beauty of its drawing, the good-hearted philosophy that reflects the soul of this gifted artist. That's why we love 'im.

Kelly's art succeeds on so many levels. It's satirical, artistic, humane, thoughtful, and screamingly funny. We miss Walt, but should feel fortunate that we have *The Complete Pogo Comics* to savor and preserve his inimitable cartoon art. Don't miss a single volume. I know I won't.

ANIMAL
COMICS
10¢
No. 15
JUNE-JULY

Albert and Pogo
ALBERT, YO' MUS' BE SICK IF YO' ISN'T WANNA GO FISHIN' FO' CATFISHES.
AH GOT A MIZ'RY— POSSIBLE AH DYIN'.

DYIN' !? MAN DAT DERE IS A BAD SICKNESS — — BAD CASE OF DYIN' PUT A MAN IN BED FO' DAYS!

OH, YASSUH – ALL OF A SUDDEN AH IS ALL COME OVER TREMBLY— POSSIBLE AH NEEDS A CATFISH SAM'WICH.
DE BAYOU BUSTIN' WIF CAT-FISHES.

TELL YOU WHUT, POGO, YO' RUSH OUT AND COTCH UP A MESS OF CATS---- AH WILL REST AND RECOVER.
SOMETIMES AH WISH US POSSUMS WAS UN-REE-FINED.

SHECKS -- POSSUMS IS LAZY FOLKS LIKE ANYBODY ELSE. BUT AH NEVAH GIT NO CHANST TO PROVE MA NATCHERAL BORN TALENTS.
SWAN OF D' SWAMP

NUFFIN' LURE IN DE FISHES LIKE A GOOD BANGIN' AN' A WHANGIN' ON DE BANG-JO.
SWAN OF D' SWAMP

POSSUM UP A 'SIMMON TREE

NOW WHAT IN THUNDER IS THAT? AH IS HEERD RACKETS IN MA TIME BUT THERE BE THE RANKEST RACKET EVAH!
GRIZZLY FLATS STREET RAILWAY.

WHATEVAH AIL THAT LAD, DOCTAH LEGERDEMAIN Z. PRESTO IS THE MAN WHAT CAN CURE HIM.

YEOW
WHUT DAT?
AHOY, THE SCOW!

ONE STEP NEARER AN' AH BUS' YO' ----WHO YO' CALL A SCOW?

THAT WAS JUS' MA NAUTICAL WAY...
WELL, AH IS CLEAN AND WHOLESOME. NEVAH HEERD NOTHIN' NAUTICAL AFORE.

BESIDES, AH IS FISHIN' AN' YO' IS DISTURBIN' ME.

A FISHERMAN! WHAT GOOD LUCK!

SPECIALLY FO' YOU! NOW WATCH VEDDY CLOSELY, MA BOY--

-THERE YOU ARE, MA BOY—A BOTTLE OF DR. LEGERDEMAIN Z. PRESTO'S ELIXIR!

HEAH IS MAN'S BES' FRIEND—A FEW DROPS MAKES A POT OF CHICKEN SOUP A TEASPOONFUL KEEPS A CHILD QUIET—IT REMOVES SPOTS—CURES CHILBLAINS AND
TWO DOSES 'LL GROW HAIR ON A WATERMELON.

AW, WHO GIVE A HOOP? AH ISN'T GOT NO WATERMELON AN' IF AH DID, AH WOULDN'T BE GROAN HAIR ON IT.
AH, YOU AH RIGHT.
AND OBSERVE THE IRRIDESCENCE OF THE TRANS-PARENCY— THAT WO'TH A DOLLAH ALONE.
BUT WHUT GOOD IS THAT FO' A FISHIN' MAN?

WHAT A KEEN YOUNGSTER YOU ARE, OLD MAN, ----THAT IS AN EXCELLENT QUESTION.

WATCH—JES' OBSERVE DE RESULT!
THE FISH WILL VERITABLY POP OUT OF THE WATAH!

DE END OB DE WORL' COMIN'—A TEERIFYIN' POISON COME SPLASH-IN' INTO DE SWAMP—US FISH AN' TURKLES IS DOOMED.

FEAR NOT, MA LI'L TURKLE PAL. THE EFFECTS WILL WEAR OFF SOON.
WHY, DAT STUFF IS MIRACULISH— AH WILL BUY A WHOLE BOTTLE, EFFEN IT DON'T COST TOO MUCH.
SWAN OF D' SWAMP

FO' YOU, MA BOY, TH' BOTTLE IS FREE IF YOU'LL JUST DO A FEW CHORES FO' ME.

ALL YO' DO IS HE'P ME SELL A FEW BOTTLES AN' AH WILL GIVE YO' ONE.

AH WILL DO IT! WHY, ANYBODY WOULD BUY DAT STUFF!

COME ON. AH WILL FIND US DE FUST CUSTOMER.
SWAN OF D' SWAMP

NOW THEN, MA BOY— WHEAH AT IS THE SUCKER— AH MEAN CUSTOMER?
OVAH CHERE.

NOW, FUST OFF YOU ENTERTAINS WITH SINGIN' AN' BANGJO WORK! THEN YOU SNEAKS A DISGUISE OUT OF DE SATCHEL AND POPS INTO IT!
AH POPS INTO DE SATCHEL?

THE DISGUISE! YO' RUNS ROUN' TO WHEAH AH IS LECTURIN' AN' BUYS A BOTTLE WIF A DOLLAH WHICH AH LEAVES IN THE SATCHEL.

THEN OUAH VICTIM—AH MEAN PROSPECT SEES YO' BUYIN' UP THIS FAKE— UH-MEDICINE IT MAKE HIM BUY IT LIKE MAD.
HOT DOG! AH IS A MEDICINE SHOW STAR.

THERE OUR BOY! EASE DE BARGE UP QUIET— HE SLEEPIN'.

YO' READY?
YASSUH.

BOORAWP!
POSSUM UP A GUMSTUMP!
WANGABLANGAWANKARANG!
BLINKAWANKARANKABLING!

YEOW!
HALP!
AH SOORENDAH! AH GIVE UP... JES' PLEASE DON'T WHUP ME!

WHY, THAT VARMINT IS GETTIN' AWAY!
YEAH— HE RUNNIN' OUT ON US AFTER WE ENNERTAIN HIM. HE A INGRATE AN' A CHEAP SKATE TO BOOT!

CHEAT *ME*, WILL YO'? AH'LL SHOW YO'.
MAN, DAT MEDICINE GOOD FO' LOTS OF THINGS.
BONK!

WHOOP! ALBERT SWALLY DE BOTTLE OF MEDICINE, DOC.!
HEAH IS A ACADEMIC BIT OF INT'REST. NEVAH SEE A MAN TAKE A WHOLE BOTTLE OF ELIXIR— SPECIAL INCLUDIN' TH' BOTTLE.
WHY, LOOKY— MRS. CRANE, AH DO B'LEEVE A MEDICAL SHOW GOIN' ON.
UG UG GLOOG!

WOOP!
DON'T BE FRIGHTED, MIS' RACKETY COON. ALBERT IS PART OF DE SHOW.
YAWP!

WHY, ALBERT IS REAL CLEVAH!
GROO!
WIP! WIP! WIP!

YASSUH— LOOKY DERE. HE KIND O' FLYIN'!
mubble!
huff huff

DALYRIMPLE! DALYRIMPLE!

WHEE-HOO! MAN, WHUT A PUFFORMINTS.

Psssssst- QUICK NOW'S YO' CHANCE TO SLIP INTO YO' DISQUISE —— AH WILL LECTURE AT THE MULTITUDE.
BUT—BUT— HOW 'BOUT ALBERT?

LET HIM DROWN! WHEN AH HIRE A BOY, HE DOES LIKE AH SAY! GO INTO YO' ACT BEFO' AH STAB YO' CROSS-EYED!
YESSUH YESSUH YESSUH YESSUH YESSUH YESSUH YESSUH

LADIES AN' FOLKS- GIVE METH' BORRY OF YO' EARS.
DAT DOC IS A FAKE AN' A FIEND. —AH GOTTA SAVE DE SWAMP PEOPLE FUM HIS POISON ELIXIR.

WHY, COUSIN DOWNWIND! AH DIN'T KNOW YOU WAS IN TOWN.
YASSUH, AH VISITIN'. WHUT GOIN' ON?

DAT NO-GOOD DOCTAH IS FLIMFLAMMIN' DE PUBLIC, AN' HE TRYIN' TO DROWN ALBERT.
HE SOUND LIKE MA TARGET FO' TONIGHT.

HEAH! WE TRICK HIM- YOU PUT ON DE DISGUISE AN' YO' BUYS A BOTTLE. AH WILL GO RESCUE ALBERT, AN' US WILL ATTACK FROM DE DERRIERE
AH PREFERS DE DIRECT APPROACH BUT AH DO IT LIKE YO' SAY.

GIVE HIM HIS OL' DOLLAH FO' TH' STUFF, DEN WHEN YO' SAY THAT IT'S AWFUL — ASK FO' YO' MONEY BACK.

NOW THEN, WHO'S THE LUCKY MAN THAT GONE PURCHASE THE FUST BOTTLE?
AH IS!

THERE YO' IS, SUH! THAT'LL BE ONE DOLLAH EVEN.
UH-HUH

AHEM! THAT WILL BE ONE DOLLAH!
Phoooeee!

DAT IS DE WUST SMELL AH EVER SMELT! AN' AH IS A EXPERT— AH DEMAND DE RETURN OF MA DOLLAH!

YO' IS A DIRTY DOUBLE-CROSSAH! WHEAH'S MAH DOLLAH?
Y'ALL HEAH DE MAN? HE CROOKED! HE CHEATIN' A PO' OL' MAN OUT OF HIS LIFE SAVIN'S.
DOCTAH, YO' IS A THIEF!
YOU AWFUL!

VERY WELL, KINDLY STEP THIS WAY, SUH. THE MANAGEMENT BE GLAD TO MAKE A SETTLEMENT!
GIVE DE OL' MAN HIS MONEY.

NOW, FRIENDS, AH WILL SHOW Y'ALL THAT THIS HEAH IS A FAKE - A FRAUD - A CHEAT - A HUMBUG A DOUBLE-DEALER AND A-

SKUNK IF EVER AH SEEN ONE!
MA WORD! AH IS TELLIN' THE HONEST TO BETSY TROOF! YOU IS A SKUNK!
MM-HMM - DAT'S DE WAY IT IS WIF ME.

HALP!
JES' A MINUTE, FOLKS – DE DOC AN' ME IS GOIN' INTO CONFERINSTANCE.

THERE'S TH' DOC'S BOAT, ALBERT, WE GONE SNEAK UP SOOROUND HIM!
AH GONE WHOP HIM.
SWAN OF

YEOW—NOT THAT- NO NO-OH DON'T—WOWF!
HALP
HURRY UP, ALBERT, DAT FIEND GOT PO' DOWN-WIND.

GANGWAY!

WHUT IN DE WORL' WAS DAT DERE?
DAT WAS YO' ASSOCIATE, DR. LEGERDEMAIN Z. PRESTO.
YEOW

HOT DOG–AH MADE A WHOLE DOLLAH OUTEN DE DEAL.
GOOD! BUT WHAT DID YO' DO TO DAT BOY?

WELL, YO' MOUGHT SAY AH GIVE HIM A DOSE OF HIS OWN MEDICINE!
COME ON, FOLKS, WE DONE FRY UP DE CATFISH POGO COTCH– DEY READY NOW.

ANIMAL

COMICS

Albert AND Pogo
POGO, AH IS A TIRED MAN... JES' ROW ME OVAH TO DE SHO'. AH B'LEEVE AH GONNA REST UR
YOU TIRED? F'UM WHUT?
THE CITY OF SAV

NATCHERAL AH GIT TIRED WATCHIN' YOU ROW DISH YERE SCOW ROUND DE SWAMP.

MAN, YOUR MIND EITHER ON ONE SIDE OR D'OTHER. YOU EITHER FINKIN OF YOUR STOMACH OR DREAMIN' ON YOU BACK.

AW, DE CAT-FISHES ISN'T BITIN' ANY-WAYS, POGO. COME ON AND NAP A SPELL.

AH GONE ROW DOWN DE SWAMP A WAYS AN' VISIT MA COUSIN DE BULLFROG... HE GOT A MISERY IN HES LI'L TOE.

HALP-HALP! SAVE US SWEET OL' FOLKS FUM A FEARFUL DEATH!

WHERE IS YOU AT? AH READY TO OBLIGE Y'ALL BY SAVIN' YOU LIFES, BUT A CAIN'T SEE Y'ALL.
US HERE, DROWNIN' AWAY FIT TO KILL-PO' US-NOBODY KEER!

WHOA IS ME! DE SWAMP VOICES IS GOT ME—AH IS BEIN' HAUNTED BY DE GHOSTS OF DROWNED FOLKS!

OH, SWAMP GHOSTS, AH HEARS YOU BUT CAN'T SEE YOU—IF YOU DOAN' HURT ME NONE, AH DO ANYFING YOU SAY!

STOP DE JAWIN' AN' CHUCK US SUMP'N TO FLOAT ROUN' ON... DEN YOU KIN SEE US FOLKS.
AH'S CHUCKIN' BUT AH AIN'T LOOKIN'!

DAT SOUN' LIKE POGO—YOU SPECK HE LITTLE BIT TETCHED? HE CAIN'T SEE US LI'L MICES DROWNIN' AN HE FINK WE IS GHOSTES.

DERE HE GO—POLIN' AWAY LIKE MAD... JES' WHEN WE GONE ASK HIM WHERE A PASSEL O' HOMELESS LI'L MICE KIN LIVE!
US HEADIN' FO SHO'!

LOOKY DERE—A HOLLER LOG—BIG AS LIFE AN' TWICE AS UGLY!

BOYS, WE GOT A PLACE TO LIVE... NUFFIN' LIKE HAVIN' A PLACE TO LIVE IN, I ALLUS SAY!

YASSUH, DISH IS A COZY OL' HOLLER LOG, ALL RIGHT!

HERE AH COME... PERTY SOON US SNUG AS BUGS IN DISH YERE OL' LOG!

MMMPH! SEEM AH HEAR VOICES... WHO COULD IT BE?
IT DARK!

MA SAKES—AH STILL HEARIN' DEM VOICES... MAYBE AH IS GITTIN' BLIND— CAIN'T SEE NOBODY!
SOMEBODY IS SQUOZIN' DOWN ON US!

WHO DERE?

WHO WHERE? CUT OUT DAT TWISTIN' AN' TURNIN'!
WHERE YOU HIDIN', YOU MIZZABLE SKUNKS?

STOP DAT!
GO 'WAY!
AH GONE FIND YOU IF IT TAKE ALL DAY!

COUSIN BULLFROG, AH IS JES' EXCAPED WIF MA LIFE FUM A PASSEL OF SWAMP GHOSTS!
WHY, COUSIN POGO, WE ISN'T HAD GHOSTS IN DE SWAMP FO' NIGH ONTO THUTTY YEAR!
CITY OF SAVANNAH

SO—YOU DOESN'T B'LEEVE ME! YOU OWN FLESH AN' BLOOD COUSIN?
MAN, YOU GOTTA SHOW ME. AH'S A MISSOURI MAN AT HEART.

DAT JES' DE TROUBLE, YOU CAIN'T NOT SEE DESE GHOSTS! HOO, HOO, HOO!

WHUFFO DE DEE-RISIVE LAUGHTER?
POGO, YOU KNOWS DE GOV'MINT KILL OFF ALL DE GHOSTS WHEN DEY SPRAY DE SWAMP WIF OIL FO' DE SKEETERS.

AH WILL PADDLE US BACK WHERE AH HEARS DE MYSTERIOUS VOICES! AH SHOWS YOU!
AH GO 'LONG BUT JES' FO' DE RIDE... DE BREEZE IS REFRESHIN'!
CITY OF SAVANNA

AH WAIT HERE AN' WHEN DEM INVISIBLE VOICES SHOW DEYSELFS, AH WILL POP OUT AT 'EM AN' WHOP 'EM GOOD!
KEEP YO' EARS PEELED!
AH HEARS NUFFIN WIF A CAPITAL NUFF!

DERE! DERE IS PROOF— DE OAR DEY RODE INTO SHO' ON AN' TRACKS LEADIN' FUM DE WATER AIDGE!
US GOTTA FOLLY DE TRACKS.

IF YOU IS SO BRAVE, WHY DONCHOO LEAD DE WAY?
DON'T FO'GIT MA SORE TOE!

MAN, MAN! IF AH SEES ANYTHIN' INVISIBLE, AH WILL JES' ABOUT DIE!
DAT AH GOTTA SEE! YOU SEEIN' SUMPIN' INVISIBLE!

AH HEARS SUMPIN' COMIN' AN' TALKIN'!

WHOOOSH
GOTCHA!

HALP! HALP! WE IS GOT! WE IS GOT! AH CAIN'T LOOK AT DE HORRIBLE AN' INVISIBLE FIENDS! HALP! HALP!
LEGGO ME, YOU OVERGROWED LIZARD—AH'LL POP YOU ONE!
WHUT ALL DE RUCKUS?
WHO HOLLERIN'?
DE LOG ROLLIN' ROUN' AGAIN!

AH BEG YOU PARDON, MISTAH FRAWG, BUT AH WAS POPPIN' AFTAH SOME INVISIBLE VOICES.
MAN, DAT WHUT US LOOKIN' FO' TOO!

HEY—SNAP OUT OF IT. POGO! AH GONE HELP YOU LOOK FO' DE INVISIBLE VOICES.
HALP, HALP!

YEOW!
YOU IS EVEN MO' HORRIBLE DAN AH IMAGINED!
WHY, YOU LI'L DAWG! DISH YERE'S ME, ALBERT!

TAKE IT EASY, POGO. LONG BOAT YERE HAS BEEN HEARIN' VOICES TOO... MEBBE DE SWAMP IS HAUNTED!
YEH, AN' AH IS HANDSOME, TOO!

YOU HEAR ANYFING?
WHUT'S GOIN' ON?

ALBERT, DE VOICES COME FUM INSIDE YOU!
IT DID?

COME OUT OF DERE!
WE SEEN DIS PLACE FUST—WE STAYIN'!
AH WILL WHOP YOU!

PSST—AH B'LEEVE ALBERT'S HAUNTED!
LOOK DAT WAY!

LET'S US NOT HANG AROUND CLUTTERIN' UP DE ISSUE...
AH HEARS YOU TALKIN'!

CUT DAT OUT!
HEY!

HEE, HEE—DAT TICKLES! SAY, WHERE YOU GONE, POGO?
WE LEAVIN' DE PREMISES. YOU IS HAUNTED, ALBERT!
AH IS?

WOWIE! AH CAIN'T STAND ANYFING HAUNTED—AH GITTIN' OUT OF YERE!

AH GUESS US OUTRUN DE HAUNTS.
AH GUESS SO.

WHOOP?!
WHUT'S ALL DE FUSS?
IT'S DEM AGIN.

AH DON'T B'LEEVE GHOSTS KIN HAUNT A MAN SAME AS A HOUSE!
LISTEN GOOD, POGO...SEE IF YOU KIN HEAR WHO IS DOWN DERE.
WE AIN'T MOVIN' OUT!

AH HATE TO INCINERATE DAT YOU ISN'T A GOOD HOUSEKEEPER, ALBERT, BUT AH FINK YOU GOT MICE!
AH WILL LOOK AROUND.

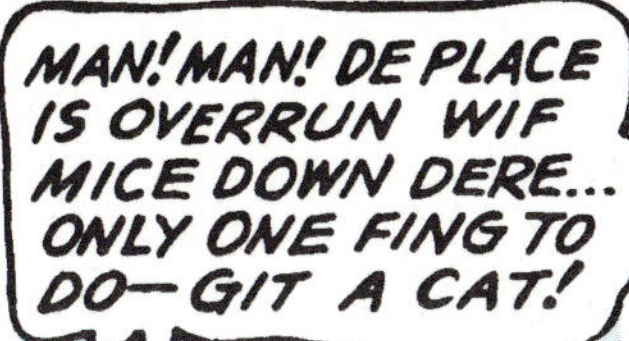
MAN! MAN! DE PLACE IS OVERRUN WIF MICE DOWN DERE... ONLY ONE FING TO DO—GIT A CAT!

LATER
DERE, ALBERT, WE GOT RAT POISON, EX-PLOSIVES AN'—
AH'D RUTHER HAVE DE MICE.

NOW WE GONE CHASE OUT DE MICE—OR ELSE!
ELSE WHUT?

ELSE WE BLOWS 'EM OUT—LOOK OUT!
POGO, DE POWDER SLIPPED. IT'S ON FIRE!

BOOM!

HOW YOU LIKE DAT, ALBERT? WE GOT RID OF YOU MICE EASY AS PIE—BUT WE BLOWED UP DE LADDER!
YEAH, HUSTLE UP AN' GIT US ANOTHER LADDER, WE WANNA GIT OUT.
AH GOT A GOOD MIND TO GO TO A SODY POP STORE AN' DROWN Y'ALL IN SARSAPARILLA.

FACT IS—MEBBE AH LEAVE YO' BOYS DOWN DERE... DO YOU GOOD!
BY JINGY, WE AIN'T GONE DO YOU NO GOOD, IF YOU LEAVES US!

MISTUH RACKETY-COON, DON'T YOU HAVE NO MO' ROPE DAN DISH YERE LI'L BITTY PIECE?
DAT'S DE ONLIEST ROPE AH GOT.

YO' REALIZE DAT MEANS POGO AN' DE FROG-BOY GOTTA STAY IN MA STOM-ACH... US CAIN'T PULL HIM OUT.
MEBBE DEY WILL DISSOLVE.

YO' TAIL, PLUS DE ROPE SHOULD REACH DEM BOYS.
WHAT'S GOIN' ON?
H'LO, PORKYPINE! WE PULLIN' POGO AN' DE FROG OUTEN ALBERT.

US WILL.
OKAY—NOW PULL HARD!
AH IS GOT A HOLT.

SWISH
!!

GEE, DAT WAS QUICK—BUT YO' BOYS ALL PULLED YO'SELVES OUTEN SIGHT!

DAT'S CAUSE POGO PULL US INSIDE!
MA SAKES, DID YO' HAFTA GIT A OL' PORKYPINE TO HELP OUT?

EV'YBODY GROSP HOLT OF DE BRANCH—AN' KEEP DAT PORKYPINE QUIET—HE HOT!

PHWOP!

NEXT TIME AH SLEEPS AH GONE PUT A WINDER SCREEN IN MA MOUF.
JES' SO WE DON' LAND ON DE PORKYPINE, AH IS SATISFIED.
DAT DE LAST TIME AH HELP OUT ALBERT BY HELPIN' OUT ANYBODY OUT OF ALBERT.
YEAH, COME ON, PORKY—MUSH OVER A LITTLE. YOU IN A BAD POSITION FO ME.

ALBERT
AND
POGO

WE IS NEAR DE PLACE, CHILLUNS... HOLE YOU HOSSES-POOTY SOON US EATS AN' RESTS OURSELVES FIT TO KILL
POGO POSSUM

HOT DOG! HERE AH IS, COMFY-TERRIBLE AN' HAPPY, WIF HARDLY A CARE IN DIS WHOLE SWEET OL' WORL'.
THEORY OF RELATIVITY

KNOCK
KNOCK
COME AWN IN! AH SETTIN'— AH CAIN'T GIT UP TO UNSHET DE DO!

COUSIN POGO, HERE IS AH— YO' NATCH'L-BAWN SECOND COUSIN!
COUSIN MARSUPIAL! YO' IS A SIGHT! FO' SORE EYES, AH MEAN!

COUSIN POGO, AH ALLUS FIGGER A FRIEN' OF YOURN IS A FRIEN' OF MINE AND VICA VERSA
ABSOLUTE KEE-RECT! US POSSUMS GOTTA STICK TOGETHER

IN DAT CASE, AH INVITES IN MAH FRIEN— COME AWN IN. PERSPY!
PERSPY?
PERSPICACITY POSSUM, DAT'S ME—A BEAUTIFUL YOUNG WIDDER WOMAN

IT SHO' IS NICE TO OFFA ME AN' MA CHILLUN A HOME... AH IS PUSSONAL VERY GRATEFUL!
PODDEN ME, MAM?

AH WHUPS IN MA TAIL AN' YOUNG PORRIDGE APPEAR—PORRIDGE IS A BRIGHT BOY—LOOK LIKE HIS PAW!
YOU GONE LIKE PORRIDGE, POGO.
WIF SUGAR AN' CREAM AH WOON'T LIKE DAT BOY!

HAUL LI'L PARASOL IN, PORRIDGE...COME AN' MEET DE GENT'MAN WHUT GIVE US A ROOF OVER OUR HAIDS.
AN' PUT FOOD IN OUR MOUFS.
BUT—BUT—

SAY LOOKY C'HERE, COUSIN MARSE! WHUFFO YOU BRING DISH PARCEL O' MOOCHERS IN YERE?
AH MOUGHT EZ WELL TELL YOU—HER AND I IS MARRIED UP DISH YERE OUAH HONEYMOONEY

YOU KNOWS DE CODE OF DE SOUTHLAND—HORSPITALITY TO ALL—NEVAH MIND WHO! DISH NEW BRIDE WOMAN O' MINE IS PRACTICAL YOU FLESH AN' BLOOD!

GOSH! WHY DIN'T Y'ALL REMAIN WHERE YOU WAS AT?
'CAUSE DE WIDDER WAS LIVIN' IN A VIRGINNY WOODPILE 'LONG COME A COLD VIRGINNY WINTER AN'—

POOF! DE WIDDER IS DISPOSSESS! NATCHERAL AH PROTECTS HER F'UM DERE ON! WE HAID RIGHT FO' YOU PLACE! AH IS A GENT'MAN WHUT KNOW HIS DUTY.
SNAP!

GUESS AH MOUGHT AS WELL RESIGN MASE'F—AH'LL GO WHUP 'EM UP A POT OF TEA AN' A FEW COOKIES.

AH GUESS IT MUS' BE TUFF TO BE A WIDDER WOMAN—HOPES AH NEVAH IS
COOKIE

YOWTCH!
CRUNCH!
COOKIES

JES' KEEP OUTEN DE COOKIES, UNCLE POGO—AH SEED UM FUST AN' AH IN YERE CHOMPIN' 'EM!
COOKIE

AH BETTER PUT SUMP'N ON DAT FINGER—MMM DAT BOY GOT TEEF LIKE A CROSS-CUT SAW!

OUT! OUT! NO NEED TO INVADE A LADY'S PRIVATE BAFF!
'SCUSE ME, PERSPY!

ONLY FING AH GITS TO DO ROUN'CHERE IS LAY IN MA BED WIF A SUFFERIN' FINGAR BONE.

NEVAH DISTURB SLEEPIN' CHILLUNS—AN' DAT'S WHAT AH IS!
KLOONK!

DAT SETTLE IT—AH GONE OFF AN' LEAVE DISH PEST HOUSE...AH IS A LONG-SUFFERIN' MAN, AN' PATIENT TO BOOT, BUT DISH YERE IS TOO MUCH!

AN' JES' TO BE ON THE SAFE SIDE, AH GONE DISGUISE MASELF.

POGO POSSUM
WHEN DEY MOVES, AH COMES BACK AN FOOMERGATES DE PLACE.

G'BYE, ALBERT.
G'BYE.

GOODBYE? SHECKS, AH DIDN'T NEVAH SEEN DAT BOY BEFO' IN MA LIFE!

MA SAKES, MEBBE AH IS SEEIN' FINGS!

H'LO, POGO!
UMPF!

POGO? DAT BOY MUS' BE SHRINKIN'!

SUMPIN'S WRONG!
DIN'T SEE POGO, HUH, PARASOL?
NOPE! AH IS GOIN' BACK.

HEY, POGO, WHAT'S GOIN' ON? SAY, YOU IS GETTIN' SMALLER!

SPEAK TO ME, POGO! HOW COME YOU IS SHRINKIN?

AH DON'T SPEAK TO STRANGERS!
PLINK!

DAT SETTLE IT! AH GOIN' TO GIT TO DE BOTTOM OF DISH YERE MYSTERY.

AH GONE GIT INTO MA DETECTIN' OUTFIT.
ALBERT ALLIGAT

WHENEVER A MYST'RY COME UP, SHADDRACK HOMES ALLIGATOR IS MA NAME.

AH WILL START RIGHT AT POGO'S HOUSE INVESTIGATIN' DISH YERE RUCKUS.

WHUT YOU WANT? AN' WHUT ON EARTH IS YOU?
AH FROM SCOTLAND YARD, SONNY-WHERE POGO?

DAT NO-GOOD DONE DISAPPEAR!
WHUT?

WOE IS ME-DAT PORE LITTLE FELLA FINALLY SHRINKED TO DE VANISHIN' POINT!

MA BES' FRIEND GONE! POOF-LIKE DAT...MUST OF BEEN A BAD CASE OF DE DWINDLES—DWINDLED OFF TO NUFFIN!

UNLESS IT WAS DE BLACK HAND OF YOU DERE, STRANGER!
WHUT?

AH POINTS DE FINGERBONE OF SUSPICION AT YOU, MA MAN! POGO DONE VANISH—HE SICKEN OFF AND GRADUAL DISAPPEAR!
HMMM...

DON'T HMMM AT ME, BOY! YOU IS RESPONSIBLE! YOU GIVED HIM A CASE OF DE DWINDLES...YOU IS A VOODOO!

OF CO'SE POGO DISAPPEARED, AN' AH IS DE VOODOO DAT PUT DE SPELL ON HIM—AN' AH WILL FIX YOU TOO!
BUT AH IS PURE AN'—

REMEMBER ALL DEM THINGS YO' BORRIED F'UM POGO, ONE TIME OR 'NUTHER?
OH, AH DO!

NOW DERE WAS A FISHIN' REEL, A OL' ROWBOAT, TWO JARS OF HARD CANDY, A PICTURE OF SAVANNAH 'FO' DE WAH, AND FO' HUNDRED DRIED OFF BUSTERFLY WINGS.
MAN, YOU IS A MIND READER!

ALSO, DEY WAS A FOAMINGRAPH WIF RECORDS AN' A LONG MOWER!

BY JING, YOU IS A HOTHEAD FO' DIGGIN' UP DE PAST... DE LONG MOWER AH BORROW DURIN' DE DEPRESSION AH 'MEMBER... AH WAS GONE INVENT A COMBINATION SNOW PLOW, COPPIT BEATER AN' LONG MOWER, BUT DE BIG TRUSTS DONE FROZE ME OUT.

AN' AH 'MEMBERS WHUFFO' YOU BORRY DE FOAMINGRAPH... IT HAD A RECORD OF MISS LILY LANGTRY, DE JERSEY LILY, SINGIN' LIKE A ANGEL.
OH, YASSUH! SHE MA FIRS' LOVE!

'MEMBER DISH YERE? BILLY BONES USETA SING IT ON DE REVERSE SIDE O' MISS LANGTRY...
OH, MOTHER DEAR, I WILL BE TRUE, TRUE TO THE PROMISE I MADE.
I'LL NEVER LET YOU DOWN, MA, FOR I WILL NEVER FAIL!
OH, GULP! MAN, DAT POGO'S FAVRIT SONG.

TONIGHT I'LL COME WHEN IT'S GROWN DARK! TONIGHT I'LL NEVER QUAIL...

I'LL SAW THE BARS AND HELP YOU OUT OF THAT OLD GREY STONE JAIL!
MAN! MAN! DAT WAS PERTY. WE ALLUS COULD SING GOOD BOFE AT DE SAME TIME AN' TOGETHER, POGO!
US SHO' COULD AND DO!

BUST MA BUNIONS! YOU IS POGO, YOU ISN'T NO VOODOO! WHAT KIND OF FLIM FLAM IS YOU FLIMMIN', POGO?
AW, SHECKS! YOU COTCHED ME!

AH WHISPER DE TROUBLES AH IN... BUZZ-HUMF-BOOPS WUZZUMMUFF ATOOF A-MPH SCIBBER WIZ-SP-WIP!
NO FOOLIN!?

WHY DON'T YOU TH'OW DE INVADERS OUT? DEY IS ENROACHIN' ON YOU' PRESARVES! BE A MAN, YOU LI'L DOPE, LIKE A REG'LAR POSSUM!
BUT! YO' FO'GITS DE CODE OF DE SOUTH.

REMEMBAH! NEVAH REFUSE HOSSPITALERY TO NOBODY NOT EVEN IF DEY IS RELATIVES.
YOU IS RIGHT! NOW LOOKY YERE, MA MAMMY DONE TOLE ME SUMPIN!

SHE SAY, "ALBERT, A BOY GOTTA BE HANDSOME OR REAL SWEET TO SUCCEED." NATCHERAL AH IS HAN'SOME SO AH NEVAH HAD TO BE VERY SWEET!
NATCHERAL.
BUT YOU GOTTA BE SWEET—SO IF YOU TREATS DESE VISITORS VERY NICE, DEY GON TAKE PITY AN' MOVE OUT—NATCHERAL!
MM...

LOOKY—DEM FOLKS IS IN DERE GLOOMIN' DEY HEARTS OUT. DEY FINK YOU DONE VANISH FUM A BAD CASE OF DE DWINDLES.
AH AIN'T GONE CHEER 'EM UP NONE.
POGO POSSUM

BUT YOU SHOULD—YOU SHOULD BUST DEY HEARTS WIF HOSPITALLERY... WHY NOT SING DEM A COUPLE CHORUSES OF DE POSSUM PAPA'S PRAYER?
AH WON'T DO IT.

YOU IS LETTIN' DOWN DE SWAMPLAND! AH IS GREVIOUS HURTED!
VERY WELL, SINCE YOU INSISTS, AH WILL SING A LI'L BIT OF "DE MELANCHOLY MUSHRAT."

DERE WAS A MUSHRAT NAME OF MOSE STRUCK A FANCI-FOOLISH POSE HIT HIS HAID UPON HIS TOES, DISH MELONCHOLY MUSHRAT!

ONE DAY HE CLUMB INTO A TREE WHERE WAS A BEE HE DIDN'T SEE, BUT HE FELT DAT BUNGLE BEE, DISH....

WHUT ON EARTH IS DAT GHASTLY AND WEIRDLY HOWLIN?
WHY, IT'S POGO!
POGO? AH DON'T SEE HIM, NOR DO AH HEAR NUFFIN'—YO'ALL KNOWS POGO DAID OF DE DWINDLES!
...DISH MELANCHOLY MUSHRAT!

DASH ENOUGH FO' US—SEEIN' GHOSTS AN LIVIN' IN A DWINDLE CONTAMINATED HOUSE IS TOO MUCH—GOO' BYE!
OL' MUSHRAT MOSE, HE QUICKLY RENDAH HIS UN-CORN-DISH-INAL SOO-RENDAH, AND DAT, BOYS, IS DE TRULY END O' DISH MELANCHOLY MUSHRAT!
OH, MAN ALIVE! US IS STAMPEDE DE AUDIENCE!
OH, WE IS GOOD! AIN'T NO TWO WAYS ABOUT IT!

DEC.-JAN., NO.18

# ANIMAL comics

# ALBERT and POGO

GIT A HOLT OF DE BRANCH, WEEVIL, AH WILL SAVE YO'!
IT TOO FAR AWAY.

AH WILL RUSH OFF AN' GIT OL' ALBERT TO COME SWIM AFTER YO' AN' SAVE YO'!

HURRY UP! AH IS DRIFTIN' TO MA DOOM!
AH IS HOT-FOOTIN' OFF ON A ERRAND OF MERCY.

MOUGHT JES' AS WELL READ ME SOME OF DE BOOK, MEANWHILE.
Magic Tricks

BLESS MASELF! THIS YERE IS A BOOK FO' DOIN' MAGICAL TRICKLES!

NOW, FO' PLAIN DISAPPEARING, SHE SAY WIGGLE ONE HAND, TOUCH DE TOP OF YO' HAID...

JUMP IN DE AIR AN' SAY—

POZZA MOZZA WOBBLE DEEDAY!
AH CAIN'T B'LEEVE MA EYES! AH IS UNDIVISIBLE! AH CAIN'T SEE MASE'F!

HURRY UP, ALBERT, US GOTTA SAVE DE WEEVIL!

HE DOWN DERE DRIFTIN' TO HES DOOM— DONE CARRIED AWAY BY A BOOK!

SHECKS, JES' WHEN AH WAS GETTIN' GOOD AT DE "WASH-BOARD BLUES"!

HERE WE IS. MISTUH WEEVIL, DONE COME TO SAVE YO' F'UM A FATE WUSS DAN—

WEEVIL, YO' IS GONE!

SEE NO WEEVIL, HEAH NO WEEVIL, SPEAK NO WEEVIL, EH, POGO? HYUK, HYUK!
HOW KIN YO' BE FRIVVLE-NESS?

HOW KIN YO' BE GAY AN' CAREFREE WHEN OL' WEEVIL OUT DERE DROWNED, POSSIBLE?
AH IS A LOVER OF MUSIC AN' DAT MEAN AH IS A TENDER SOUL.

AH WILL WADE OUT AN' LOOK UNDERNEAF DE BOOK... HE PROB'LY HIDIN' UNDER DERE.
HURRY UP, ALBERT!
POOT

DON'T SEE NOBUDDY... HE GONE HOME, POGO — LISTEN AT DIS UNDERWATAH BLUE NOTE.
AH JES' BOUT HANGIN' ON.
PTZZPUSZX!

WHOA IS ME! AH IS A CRIMINAL! DONE SENT A MAN TO HIS DEATH!

WHUT DE BOOK ABOUT, POGO?
HELLO, POGO!
SPAP!
MAGIC TRICKS

YOWP! DE BOOK TALKIN'!
OOF! POGO, YOU OUGHT TO OF COTCHED ME!
PLOP!

WHUT YOU MEAN DE BOOK IS TALKIN'?
SHE SAY, "H'LO, POGO!"

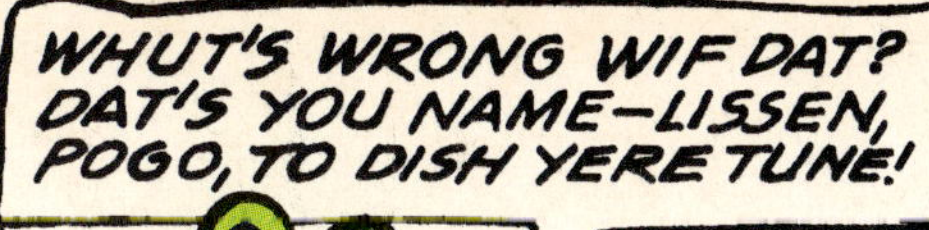
WHUT'S WRONG WIF DAT? DAT'S YOU NAME—LISSEN, POGO, TO DISH YERE TUNE!

PLAY "SWAMP STOMP," ALBERT.
MAGIC TRICKS

AH DIN'T KNOW YO' WAS A MUSIC LOVER, POGO.
DE BOOK RE-QUEST DAT NUMBAH, NOT ME!

DE BOOK GOT GOOD TASTE.
OH, DE SWAMPLAND STOMP IS DE STOMP FO' ME! IT'S JES DE TUM TIDTUM DE DE TUM...
HMMPH—DON'T EVEN KNOW DE WORDS!
MAGIC TRICKS

MA SAKES! YO' IS A VERY INTELLIGENT BOOK! WHUT IS YO' ABOUT?
OH, AH IS ALL ABOUT MAGIC.
HMMPH.
MAGIC TRICKS

FO' INSTANCE, PUT ONE HAND ON YOU HAID, AN' WIGGLE DE OTHER HAND.
LIKE DISH YERE?
HMMPH!
MAGIC TRICKS

VERY GOOD, NOW, JUMP IN DE AIR!
MAGIC TRICKS

POZZA MOZZA WOBBLE DEE DAY!
LIKE DISH YERE?
YOWP!
MAGIC TRICKS

MA SAKES! AH IS ACTUAL DISAPPEARED!
YASSUH!
HMMM!
MAGIC STUFF

AH SEES DE LIGHT! ONE SIDE, MISTUH SEE-NO-WEEVIL!
HEY, BE KEERFUL!

?
NOW, AH IS CUSTODIAN OF DE BOOK—AN' YO' BOFE IN MA POWER!
?

HEY, CAPTAIN CHURCHY LA FEMME, COME OVER YERE!

OL' ALBERT AN' DE WEEVLE IS UNVISIBLE!
IS YO' CRAZY, POGO?

NOSSUH, DEY DID A TRICK LIKE DISH YERE, DEN DEY JUMP IN DE AIR AN' HOLLER—

POZZA MOZZA WOBBLE DEE DAY!

AN' DE HUMOROUS PART—DERE DEY IS ALL UNVISIBLE AN' DON'T KNOW DE TRICK OF GITTIN' BACK!

DOES YOU KNOW?

NO, BUT AH DON'T GOTTA KNOW— HO, HO, HO!

MAN, YOU IS DE UNVISIBILLEST THING EVAH AH SEE!

AH IS?

OH MAN! POGO DONE FAINTED AN' AH CAIN'T SEE HIM TO REVIVE HIM!
PLOP!

AH GOTTA GIT HE'P! NO TWO WAYS ABOUT IT!

H. OWL
HEY, HOWLAND OWL, YOU KNOWS ABOUT VOODOO! COME ON OUT—US NEEDS YOU!

YASSUH, AH IS A VOODOO EXPERT.
US GOT A 'MERGENCY CASE-HURRY UP!
WHUT SEEM TO BE DE TROUBLE, CAPTAIN CHURCHY?
DERE IS ALBERT, AN' POGO, AN' MISTUH WEEVIL . . . DEY IS UNVISIBLE, AND US GOTTA MAKE 'EM REAPPEAR.
YASSUH.
YASSUH.
YASSUH.
WELL, LET'S SEE . . . FOUR OVER FIVE DIVIDED BY A WATERMELON MAKES A LOGARITHM.
NOTHIN' SHOWIN' UP YET.
WELL, WE PUTS DE HYPOTENOOST OVER DE HIPPOPOTAMUS AND DIVIDE BY DE HYPODERMIC.
?
DE ANSWER TO DAT IS HALF A POUND OF GRAPE FRUITS.
WHY, MAN, YOU CAIN'T VOODOO YOU WAY OUT OF A PAPER SACK! LET'S LOOK IN DE MAGIC BOOK FO' DE ANSWER.
WE RECONSTRUCKS DE CRIME FUST! HOW DISH YERE HAPPEN?
DEY PUTS ONE HAND OVER DE HAID, WIGGLE DE OTHER—
LIKE DISH?
DAT'S RIGHT, AND NOW JUMP IN DE AIR AND HOLLER—
POZZA MOZZA WOBBLE DEE DAY!
LIKE DISH?
WHUT IN TUNKET IS ALL DE HOOTIN' AND HALLOWIN' DOWN YERE, MISTUH TURKLE?
HOW YOU GIT INTO DE SWAMPLAND HAOUN' DAWG? AH GLAD TO SEE YO', HOWSOMEVER.

ALBERT, POGO, MISTUH WEEVIL AN' DE OWL IS ALL UNVISIBLE... IF YOU KIN READ, LOOK IN DISH YERE MAGIC BOOK AN' GIT ME DE ANSWER FO' MAKIN 'EM REAPPEAR.
AH KIN READ BUT AH DON'T B'LEEVE IN MAGIC SO AH DON'T THINK IT'LL WORK.
MM, DIS LOOK LIKE DE THING... IT SAY, WHISTLE ONCE, DEN STAN' ON ONE FOOT AND HOLLER—
MAGIC TRICKS
LIKE DISH—? TWEEEEET
DAT'S RIGHT... NOW AH WILL HOLLER—
HIPPITY HOPPITY LOPPITY SKOPPITY!
YOWP!
HOT DOG! YOU IS SAVED OUR LIFES, HAOUN' DAWG!
WE ALMOST FLATTENED HIM OUT!
AH IS RECOVERIN' NOW.
FO' GOODNESS SAKES, WHO IS YOU?
AH IS A FELLOW WHAT DISAPPEARED TWO YEARS AGO...
AN' SINCE AH OWNS DIS MAGIC BOOK, AH WILL NATURAL TAKE IT HOME WIF' ME.
INGRATE!
ALL DAT TROUBLE FO' NOTHIN'!

FEB.-MARCH, NO. 19

# ANIMAL comics

ALBERT and Pogo
ZOOOOOO—

WHO WAS DAT WHUT ZOOMED AT US, POGO?
A PUFFICK STRANGER TO ME, ALBERT.

HE MOUGHT BE A STRANGER, BUT HE AIN'T SO PUFFICK
WHY, HE A BIG OL' INSECK!
HMMMM DMMMMM

WHAT A DUMP! SO THIS IS THE SUNNY SOUTH! THE JOINT IS JUMPIN' WITH SOLID BOREDOM.

OH, WELL! C'EST LA GUERRE, AS THEY SAY IN PATERSON. A JERSEY MOSQUITO HAS A LOT OF BOUNCE.

I'LL DIG UP SOME CATS AROUND THIS STICK FACTORY AND SEND 'EM WITH SOMETHIN' CONCRETE AND TORRID.

JUS' A MINUTE DERE, BUG! WHERE AT YO' FINK YO' GOIN?
OH, BROTHER! GET THAT SUCCOTASH ACCENT! WHUFFO YO' WANNA KNOW, JACKSON?

MA NAME AIN'T JACKSON—AH IS ALBERT—ALBERT DE WELL KNOWN ALLIGATOR.
AN ALLIGATOR! YOU?!

YASSUH, AH IS A NATCHERAL BORN AN' HAN'SOME ALLIGATOR OF DE FUST WATER.
WHO IS YOU?
ME? I'M CITRONELLA JONES, THE SHARPEST SKEETER IN 48 STATES.

DASH WHUT US GITS FO' NOT PUTTIN' DE SCREENS UP IN DISH YERE SWAMP.
WHAT DO THEY CALL YOU WHEN THEY AIN'T LAUGHIN'?

AH IS PONCE DE LEON MONTGOMERY COUNTY ALABAMA GEORGIA BEAUREGARD POSSUM.
YOU SOUND LIKE A HEP TRAIN ANNOUNCER

OR POGO FO' SHORT.
POGO FO' SHO'TNIN' BRAID? HESH MA MOUF!

HEAR DAT ACCENT? DE BOY IS A NORTHERN MAN.

LOOK YERE, CITRONELLA JONES, YO' KIN JES' NATCHERALLY GO BACK TO TH' NORTH AN' BUZZ AROUND!
US DON'T WANT NO MO' BIG INSECKS–US GOT ENUFF NOW!

LISSEN! I'M TAKIN' OVER THIS SWAMP–IN A WEEK I'LL MUSCLE YOU ALL OUT!

YOU THINK YOU'VE HAD SKEETER BITES BEFORE? YOU'LL HAVE TO SCRATCH MINE WITH A RAKE!

WHY, DAT NO 'COUNT BUG! AH GOT A GOOD MINE TO BUY ME A SPRAY GUN!
WELL, SKEETERIN' IS HIS TRADE, ALBERT. YO' GOTTA EXPECK HE'LL SKEETER IF HE KIN.

AN' FEUDIN' IS MA PERFESSION! DAT BUG DONE MET HIS MATCH! AH WILL DOOL HIM TO DE DEATH!
BUT FINK OF DE JOY SKEETERS GIVES YO'. AH ALLUS ENJOYS SCROTCHIN' SKEETER BITES. DEY IS SUM'FING RESTFUL 'BOUT IT.

MAN. AH JES' LOVES SCRUNCHIN' AN CRUNCHIN', AN SKRITCHIN' AN' ITCHIN' AN SCROOTCHIN' AN'...

BUT IF DAT BOY BITE YOU, YOU'LL SWOLE UP AN' POP! HE'LL RAISE BUNGLES BIG ENOUGH TO SELL FO' WATAH-MELON!
YO' IS RIGHT!

HOWSUMEVAH, AH LOVES WATAHMELON, TOO.

US BEIN' BRAINY, WE SHOULD THINK OF SOME FEARLESS BUT SAFE WAY OF DOIN' AWAY WIF DAT INTRUDER!

AH IS GOT IT!

POGO, YOU IS DE COURAGEOUS DEFENDER OF OUR SHORES!
YASSUH!

POGO, MA BOY, AH IS PROUD OF YOU—AH ALLUS KNEW YO' WAS A RECKLESS GAY FIGHTIN' FOOL!
'TAIN'T NOTHIN'!
BEFO' YOU KNOWS IT FOLKS WILL SAY YOU IS "DANGEROUS POGO!" POGO, DE ACE OF DE SWAMP!
YOU KIN ALLUS CALL ME PLAIN POGO.

IN YEARS TO COME AH WILL GATHER MA CHILLUNS AN' SAY, "ACE POGO WAS MA BEST FRIEND. US WAS BOYS TOGETHER! HE DE BRAVEST MAN IN DE STATE!"
AW, SHECKS!

DASH WHY AH IS TETCHED—YO MA BEST PAL: MA BUDDY, MA CHUM; MA BOOM COMPANION, WHUT WILL NEVER LET ME DOWN!
DON'T FEEL BAD, ALBERT.

NOT FEEL BAD WIF YOU FACIN' DEATH DIS WAY?
WHUT WAY?

WHY, YOU IS ABOUT TO SAVE DE SWAMPLAND!
AH IS?

YOU IS GWINE CHALLENGE DE SKEETER AN' SETTLE DISH YERE DOOL.

BUT ISN'T IT YOUR DOOL?

DAT'S DE BEST PART OF BEIN' BUDDIES. AH SHARES DE DOOL WIF YOU!
FO'TUNATE ME!

WHUT IS MOST REMARKABLE, YOU GWINE BEAT HIM AT HIS OWN GAME!
YOU MEAN BY BITIN' FOLKS?

NOSSIR! YOU GONE OUT-FLY HIM— YOU A FIGHTER PILOT.
H·OWL

AND HOWLAND OWL IS DE MAN TO INSTRUCK YO'—
HEY OWL!

WHUT YO' WANTS, ALBERT?

US WANTS YOU TO FLY ROUND WIF POGO—HE GONE TO FIGHT A DOOL.

MM—FER A FLYIN' DOOL POGO WILL NEED A MAN WIF A STRONG WING AND A WEAK HAID—SOMEBODY LIKE—MM—MM—

AIG HAID NOONAN, DE WOOD DUCK!
DE VERY MAN!
WHUT'S SO VERY 'BOUT DAT BOY?

MISTUH NOONAN, YOU IS A VERY LUCKY MAN— YOU IS BEEN SEE-LECTED BY OUR COMMITTEE TO ACT AS PURSUIT SHIP NO. ONE.
YOU IN LINE FO' INNERNATIONAL HONORS!

AH IS PROUD, GENTMINTS; PROUD, PLEASED AND PUFFICKLY AMAZED!
MEET MR. NOONAN, POGO, HE GONE BE YOU AIRPLANE.
HE LOOK SORTA PUNY.

LOOKY DERE! MISTUH CITRONELLA JONES CIRCLING AROUND OVER HAID.

I'LL DROP THIS MUD BOMB ON THOSE BOYS, JUST TO LET 'EM KNOW I STILL CARE.

PLOP!

WIMMENS AND CHILLUNS ISN'T SAFE—AH WILL RIDE UP ON MISTUH NOONAN AND WHUP DAT BOY OUTEN DE SKY!

LET'S GO, AIG HAID NOONAN!

HAPPY LANDIN'S!
HE HAVIN' TROUBLE WIF DE TAKEOFF.
YOU ISN'T GONE TO CLEAR DE RUNWAY!
AH KNOW WHUT AH DOIN'.

FLUMP!

AH THOUGHT YOU KNEW WHUT YOU WAS DOIN'!
AH DID KNOW! AH ALLUS BUNKS INTO STUFF... DAT'S WHY AH HATE TO FLY—AH ALLUS BUST MA HAID!

WHY DON'T US CLIMB A TREE—YOU JUMPS OFF AN' START FLAPPIN'... DEN YO' WILL BE FLYIN'.
SO AH WILL.

AH NEVER BEEN UP SO HIGH IN MA LIFE.
ME NEITHER.

AH WILL HELP YOU FLAP WHEN US GITS OFF DE LIMB.
DAT'S NICE.

WHEE!

YOU FLYIN' FINE, MISTUH AIG HAID.

SPLOP!

AH SUTTINLY ADMIRE YO' FLYIN', MISTUH NOONAN—YO FIGGER AH KIN STOP HELPIN' YOU FLAP NOW?

SHIP, YOU DONE DEE-SERT YOUR PILOT!
AH GITS AIRSICK.
YO' AIN'T HAD NO NAVY TRAININ'!

POGO FLYIN' PERTY GOOD—BUT HE'LL NEVER MAKE A GOOD BUTTERFLY.

GIMME A HAND, OWL.

DERE! DAT'S A ANNIE-AIR-CRAFT GUN FO' TO PROTECT POGO.
SHO', OL POGO SO BUSY FLYIN' HE CAIN'T FIGHT OFF DE SKEETER.

WHEN DE SKEETER SHOW UP, AH CUTS DE ROPE.

DEN UP FLIES DE MUD BALL AND BOPS DE SKEETER—BUT FUST AH BETTER FIGGER DE RANGE OUT.

YOU BETTER START FIGGERIN', HOWLAND, 'CAUSE DERE COMES CITRONELLA JONES.

AH HATE TO SAY IT, BUT AH FINK AH IS UP YERE **ALL ALONE!**

AH ISN'T SO MUCH ALONE AS AH IS WIFOUT SUPPORT.
WELL, RUFFLE MY HAIR AND CALL ME BOYISH! YOU'RE FLYIN'!

OF COURSE! AH IS A FLYIN' POSSUM NAME OF POGO.
DO ALL YOU CHARACTERS FLY?

NOPE, JES' ME... AH IS TALENTED.
YOU'RE PRETTY COCKY FOR A SQUARE.
STOP SHOWIN' OFF!
AH ISN'T SHOWIN' OFF, AH IS PRACTICIN'!

BUT IF IT'S TROUBLE YOU WANTS—PUT UP YOU DUKES!
WHY, YOU—!

OOPS—AH FO'GOT YOU WAS A NATURAL BORN SKEETER!
SWISH
MISSED HIM!

I NEVER MISS TWICE!

AH QUICK PULLS OFF MA JACKET—FLYIN' WIF MA FEETS MEANWHILE.

NOW AH WILL USE IT LIKE A CAPE.

HERE COME DE CHARGE OF DE WILD BULL.

A PERFECK PATE DE FOIS GRAS, AS US SAYS IN BULL FIGHTIN'!

LOOKY DERE! OL' POGO DONE TRAP DE SKEETER INTO DE TREE!
US FIGGERIN' DE RANGE FO' DE GUN, ALBERT.

NOW US KIN FIRE DE GUN—DE RANGE IS FOURTEEN HECTAGONALS PLUS A MESS OF OPTIONAL FRACTIONS.

SO NATURAL DAT MAKES IT SIX DAYS TO DE MINUTE PLUS FRIDAY SO DEN WE SUBDIVIDES DE PROPERTY AN'—

WE CUTS DE ROPE!

PLOOTCH!

AH SHOT MA BUDDY!
WUMP!

POGO WON DE PURPLE HAID! HE SO BRUISED HE LOOK LIKE A PLUM.

I'M GOIN' BACK TO PATERSON. THE SWAMP IS TOO TOUGH!
MAN! US WILL HAFTA SCROTCH MA SKEETER BITE IN RELAYS.
HE DIN'T LIKE YO FLAVOR, ALBERT!

APRIL- MAY, NO. 20

# ANIMAL comics

ALBERT and Pogo
MAN! MAN! IT SHO' NUFF IS A SHO' NUFF DAY FO' CATCHIN' SHO' NUFF CAT FISHES, SHO' NUFF!
SHO' NUFF!

CAST OFF DE LINES, CAPTAIN ALBERT, US GONE VENTURE ONTO DE PLACID SURFACE OF DISH YERE PRIMEVAL SWAMP AND BASK IN DE GLORY OF DE SOUTHLAND SUN.
MAN ALIVE, POGO! YO' SOUNDS LIKE A MIAMI BEACH BARKER BOY.
THE JACKSONVILLE QUEEN

WELL, AH WAS PRACTICIN' UP FO' BEIN' DE CHAMBAH OF COMMAS HERE—SEEM LIKE EV'Y BIG TOWN IN DE COUNTRY HAVE A BUNCH O' BOOSTERS.
THE JA SONVILLE QUEEN

SO AH IS WRIT SOME ADVERTISEMENT LETTERS AN' SENT 'EM OFF TO FOLKS TO COME VISIT US IN DE CLIMES OF DE SUNNY OL' SWAMPLAND.

WHY, AH DUNNO 'BOUT DAT—US'LL HAVE ALL KINDS OF RIFF RAFF FLIM-FLAMMIN' US RIGHT AND LEFT!
WHERE IS YOU SENSE OF HORSEPARTILLERY, DE WATCHWORD OF DIXIE?

AH DON'T APPROVE OF INVITIN' IN A BUNCH OF FURRINERS.
WHY, MAN, WE'LL BE MILLYUM-AIRES FUM DE REVENOO DEM BRINGS IN!
THE JACKSONVILLE

AHA! AH KNEWED IT! YOU IS A TRAITOR TO DE SWAMPLAND—YOU IS BRINGIN' IN A BUNCH OF REVENOOERS!
OOP! AH GOT A BITE!

OOOH, DIS GROSS INGRATITUDE ON YOU' PART IS A MOST GROSS INGRATEFUL ACT OF A GROSS INGRATE.

AND FURTHERMO', AH WISH TO TAKE DIS OCCASION TO— OOOGHP!
MAN! DAT'S A BIG ONE!

YOMP-OOMP-WUMP?
WHERE'S MA FISH?

ALBERT, LOOK ME IN DE EYE! WHERE'S MA FISH? AH KNOWED AH COTCHED A BIG ONE!

KOFF! KOOFF! YO' DIN'T COTCH A FISH—WHUT YOU FINK OF DAT? KOFF-KOFF!

DAT IS A BALL-FACED LIE!
THE JACKSON

DAT SETTLE IT, MISTUH POSSUM! US IS REACH DE PARTIN' OF DE WAYS... OUAH LIFELONG PARTNERSHIP IS AT A END!
AH POINTS DE FINGER-BONE OF SCORN RIGHT BACK AT YOU, MISTUH SATCHEL FACE! DON'T DARKEN MA DO' AGAIN!
THE JACKS

DAT'S DE LAS' STRAW—AH IS BEEN UNJUSTLY ACCUSE, AH IS BEEN ATTACKED, INSULTED AND REVILED **AND** BANISHED—AH IS THROUGH WIF' YO'!

HIM AN' HIS CHAMBAH OF COMMAS—AH'LL FIX DAT UP WHEN DE TIME COME!

DAWGONE—WHY DID US HAFTA GIT IN A FIGHT JES WHEN AH NEED OL' ALBERT TO HELP RUN DE CHAMBAH OF COMMAS!

HEY DERE, POGO! HEAH'S A MESS OF READIN' LETTAHS FO' YOU.
HOT DAWG! DE CLIENTS IS GONE VISIT DE SUNNY SWEET OL' SWAMPLAND, DE GEM OF CANKER COUNTY!
MALE
THE JACKS

BLESS MA CUTE LI'L OL' SELF! ALL DESE FOLKS SAY DEY COMIN' RIGHT SPANG OFF DE BAT AN' IS EXPECTIN' TO HAVE DE TIME OF DEY LIFES!
HUM!

WHUT'S GOIN' ON, POGO? WHUT DOES DAT MEAN?
DAT MEANS DAT AH GOTTA GO RECROUT MA CHAMBAH OF COMMAS.
MALE

MA SAKES! AH WONNER WHERE IS DE OWL?
AH DOWN HERE, POGO, WORKIN' OUT A PROBLEM.

AT WHUT YO' DIGGIN' AT, OWL?
AH DIGGIN' FO' A SQUARE ROOT.

AH GOT A PROBLEM WHICH SAY TAKE DE SQUARE ROOT OF THREE, DIVIDE BY DE SUPERNUMERARY AND WHUT IS DE BASIC LOGARITHM OF DE INSULATION?

WELL, IN DE FUS' PLACE, DE SQUARE ROOTS OF THREE WHUT?
JES THREE—DAT'S DE WAY US SINUSES WORK. US DON'T SPECIAL-FLY.

US BUST OUT AND SEARCH OUT DE ANSWER FO' ANYTHING WIFOUT EVER KNOWIN' WHUT'S WHUT—SOMETIMES AH FINKS AH WILL RESIGN AS A DOCTAH OF NUMBAHS AN' RUN OFF AN' BE A OPERA SINGER.

YO' WON'T FIND NO SQUARE ROOTS DOWN DERE, OWL...HERE'S A BETTER OPERA-TOONY. A MESS O' FOLKS IS COMIN' AN' AH IS ELECTIN' YOU TO MA CHAMBAH OF COMMAS.
NO FOOLIN'!

YASSUH, DEY COMIN' TO VISIT DE SUNNY LAND OF DE SWAMP, AN' US WILL ENNERTAIN 'EM.
GOOD FOR US!

MAN, US WILL FUST OF ALL TAKE DESE FOLKS ON A FISHIN' EXPOSITION...CAT FISHIN' BEIN' ONE OF DE PLEASURES OF DE SWAMP.
NATURAL.

HELLO THERE!
WHUT DAT?

DAT, AS YO' SO CRUDELY PUTS IT, IS ME—HIP-SKITCH DE HOP-FRAWG, A VISITOR TO DE SUNNY CLIME.
WHY, BLESS ME, SO IT IS—AH DIN'T EXPECT YO' TO BE SO LITTLE AN' SO EARLY.
AND SO FEW!

AH ISN'T FEW—AH BRUNGED MA CHUM, MISTUH BOWL WEEVIL. NOW DEN, WHERE AT IS DE ENTERTAINMENT?
H'LO.

OH, US IS GOT A LOVELY IDEE!
YASSUH, US GONE TAKE YOU BOYS CAT FISHIN'!
DAT'S LOVELY YET? PHOO!
PHOO!

WHUT INGRATES! CHUNK 'EM OUT OF DE SWAMP, POGO! TURNIN' UP DEY NOSES ON CAT FISHIN'!
DAT AIN'T DE WAY DE CHAMBAH OF COMMAS DO IT—US GOTTA BE HORSEPARTICIPLE... GIT ALONG, YOU BUG-YOU AND DE HOP-FRAWG GONE CAT-FISHIN' AN' GONE LIKE IT!
SHECKS!

YOU IS SHANGHAI US! WHUT WE GONE USE FO' BAIT?
US USUAL USE FOLKS LIKE YOU—SO FIGHT IT OUT BETWIX' YOU' SELFS.

BOWL, US MOUGHT AS WELL FACE IT—HERE US IS WIF A POLE MAH SIZE, SO AH GITS TO HOLD DAT! NOW WE IS LEF' WIF A HOOK WHICH IS YOUR SIZE.

SO AH GITS TO-UH—HOLD DAT?

WELL, LOWER AWAY, AND IF AH SIGHTS A CATFISH, WHUT MUS' AH DO?

STICK HIM WIF DE HOOK.

DERE DEY IS, ENJOYIN' DEYSELFS FIT TO KILL OUT DERE.
YASSUH, US IS A SUCCESS AS A CHAMBAH OF COMMAS.

WHY, OWL, US IS MADE! WE GONE WIN HUNNERDS OF FRIENDS FO DE SWAMP!
YASSUH!

HEY!
OOP!

AH IS A VISITOR TO DESE YERE PARTS, AN' AH LOOKIN' FO' DE CHAMBAH OF COMMAS WHUT IS S'POSE TO ENNERTAIN ME— SO FAR DEY DOIN' A BUM JOB!

WELL, UH—SHECKS. UH GOSH—US DON'T KNOW WHERE DE CHAMBAH IS— BUT SOME GENT-MINTS IS BEIN' ENNERTAINED DOWN IN DE SWAMPS—DEY IS CATFISHIN'!

AH'LL JOIN 'EM, BUT AH SHO' DON'T FIGGER TO ENJOY MAHSELF! AH'LL BE DOGGED IF AH LIKES CATFISHIN'!

WHUT YO' DOIN' POACHIN' ON MA PREE-SARVES, MISTUH STRANGER-FRAWG?
BEAT IT, SALAMANDER— US IS CATFISHIN'—BY COURTESY OF DE CHAMBAH OF COMMAS!

CATFISHIN', HEH!? WAL, AH HAPPENS TO BE A CATFISH! NOW WHUT?
DO YOU' DUTY, BOWL.

OUCH!

WHY, YO' LITTLE DAWGS, YOU DONE DAG ME IN DE HAND BONE!
WHUT US DO NOW WIF DIS CATFISH, HIPSKITCH?

HOT DAWG! DEY'S SOME KIND OF A RUCKUS GOIN' ON OUT DERE

DAT IS DE KIND OF ENNERTAINMENT AH LIKES!

BEAT IT, MISTUH BEAVER, DISH YERE IS A PRIVATE FIGHT!
WHO YO' FINK YO' IS?

MY GOODNESS, YO' IS A BIG BEAVER!
AH ISN'T EXACTLY A BEAVER, SON—

DAT BOY SAY HE A CATFISH!
DEN AH GONE WHOP HIM— AH DON'T LIKE CATFISHES... AFTAH DAT AH GONE WHOP YOU TWO!

NOW AH'LL JES' SET DISH YERE CATFISH UP FO' A GOOD WHOPPIN'.
AH ISN'T NO CATFISH.
US NEXT.
YO' KIN BE FUST.

MAKE UP YO' MIND— WHUT IS YOU?
AH IS A ALLIG— ALL—ALLUH— UH, OOOP! HEY-OUCH— OOOP-UH—
BUS' MA BRAIN! OL' ALBERT GITTIN' WHOPPED BY DE BEAR!

COME ON. US WILL STOP HIM—DAT BEAR CAIN'T GIT AWAY WIF DAT!
AH HAS A HUNCH HE KIN, BUT US OUGHT TO DO **SOMEFIN!**

HOLE ON DERE, BAR— YOU IS AGIN DE LAW! DE CHAMBAH OF COMMAS GOT RULES 'BOUT DISH YERE!
WHUT YO' GONE DO?

OW!
SPANK!
DIS WHUT AH DO!
DE CHAMBAH OF COMMAS BETTER LIQUIDATE ITSELF OVAHBOAD!
WHY, YOU—

STAND STILL AND AH'LL WHOP YOU WITH THIS OVERGROWED HOPPIN'-FRAWG!
JEST A MINUTE! DOWN DERE—WHUT WAS DAT LAST REMARK?
AH SAID YO' WAS A OVERGROWED HOPPIN'-FRAWG!

DAT'S WHUT AH **THOUGHT** YO' SAID, BEAR!
AND DAT'S DE ONE FING AH DON'T 'LOW MAHSE'F TO BE CALLED!
YOU FIGGERIN' ON DOIN' SUMPIN' 'BOUT IT, MISTUH OVERGROWED HOPPIN'-FRAWG?

YAS—BEAR—AH **IS** CORNSIDERIN' DE IDEE!

WOOP!
WHOP!

NOW YOU BETTER GIT 'LONG HOME, MISTUH BEAR—YOU IN DE SWAMP NOW AN' ALBERT A SWAMP 'GATOR—HE FIGHT GOOD UNNER WATER!
YASSUH!

HOT DOG! US DONE SAVE DE SWAMP F'UM A SCOURGE AGIN! US IS SHO' A POW'FUL TEAM, POGO!
YASSUH! AN' ISN'T YO' MAD AT ME ANY MO'?

NOSSUH—**YOU** WAS MAD AT **ME!**
BUT YOU STOLED MA CATFISH AN' CLAIM AH DIN'T KOTCH HIM!
LOOK OUT, BOWL! IT GONE BUST LOOSE AGIN!
THE JACK VILLE QUEEN

JES' A MINUTE—AH SHOWS YOU WHUT YO' CAUGHT!
WASN'T IT A CATFISH?

DERE'S WHUT YO' CAUGHT! CAPT'IN CHURCHY LA FEMME! HE ABSENT MINDED GRAB YO' LINE AN' YO' FLUNG HIM DOWN MA THROAT.
YASSUH! AN' LATAH AH HAD TO CLUMBER OUT OF DERE ON A LONG HANDLED STICK... NOW, COME ON AN ENJOY DE CATFISHES AH COTCHED WHILST YOU FOLKS WAS THRASHIN' ROUND—EAT HEARTY, BOYS!

# ALBERT the ALLIGATOR